S0-BNC-059

The Skinwalker Novels

In the magical middle ages, humans and Skinwalkers lived side by side. The humans had only one skin, but Skinwalkers could change from human to animal form. This difference led to problems on both sides.

Legend of the Ring *by* D.M. OUELLET Only a stable boy can head off an all-out war between humans and Skinwalkers.

Walking Both Sides *by* C.A. RAINFIELD A teenage boy shoots a Skinwalker, and soon the clans want revenge. Can a teenage girl bring peace between humans and Skinwalkers?

Wolves at the Gate *by* E.L. THOMAS A young pickpocket must flee to the huts of the Skinwalkers to avoid the King's soldiers. But that is only the beginning of his problems.

The SKINWALKER Novels

Walking Both Sides

C.A. RAINFIELD

Copyright © 2011 by High Interest Publishing, Inc.

All rights reserved. No part of this book may be reproduced or transmitted in any form or by any means electronic, mechanical, optical, digital or otherwise, or stored in a retrieval system without prior written consent of the publisher. In the case of photocopying or other reprographic reproduction, a licence from CANCOPY may be obtained.

LIBRARY AND ARCHIVES CANADA CATALOGUING IN PUBLICATION

Rainfield, C. A. (Cheryl A.)
    Walking both sides / Cheryl Rainfield.

(HIP fantasy)
(Skinwalker novels)
ISBN 978-1-926847-15-3

I. Title. II. Series: HIP fantasy III. Series: Skinwalker novels

PS8635.A433W34 2011   jC813'.6   C2011-900527-1

General editor: Paul Kropp
Text design: Laura Brady
Illustrations drawn by: Charlie Hnatiuk
Cover design: Robert Corrigan

1 2 3 4 5 6 7   15 14 13 12 11

Printed and bound in Canada by Webcom.

High Interest Publishing acknowledges the financial support of the Government of Canada through the Canada Book Fund for our publishing activities.

CONTENTS

PROLOGUE 3

CHAPTER 1: Hunting or Murder? 5

CHAPTER 2: Arrested 13

CHAPTER 3: Ambush 20

CHAPTER 4: More Revenge 29

CHAPTER 5: Curious 41

CHAPTER 6: A Battle 53

CHAPTER 7: Too Many Dead 61

CHAPTER 8: Mistrust 69

CHAPTER 9: Running Away 75

CHAPTER 10: The Mob 83

CHAPTER 11: Bewitched? 90

CHAPTER 12: The Fire 97

For Jean, who helped me find happiness
for my own story.

And for everyone who loves to lose
themselves in a good story.

Prologue

At the dawn of the first forest, clans of Skinwalkers and One-Skins lived side by side. Sometimes the Skinwalkers walked in their animal skins. Sometimes they walked in their human skins. Sometimes they settled on the in-between. One-Skins, the humans, were their friends.

But that was long ago. Over centuries, the One-Skins became more powerful. Some thought that Skinwalkers were evil. Some told stories of Skinwalker magic. Then, under the iron rule of King Rudgerd, soldiers began to hunt and kill Skinwalkers. Now the few remaining clans must live in hiding.

But all that is about to change. A teenage boy, a One-Skin, kills a Skinwalker while hunting. This murder sets off a battle between Skinwalkers and One-Skins that can bring disaster to both sides.

The only person who can bring peace is a girl. A girl who must stand between both sides and fight for justice.

CHAPTER ONE | Hunting or Murder?

Claire's stomach tightened in hunger. She held her bow and arrow ready to bring down some game. But it had been a hard winter. There still weren't many animals about.

It was spring. The forest should be full of rabbits and squirrels, but the forest felt empty. Claire had never seen it like this before. Her grandfather said he'd seen harder winters, but Claire didn't remember one. Never had they been so hungry.

Claire looked at her cousin, Kelsey, beside her. Kelsey

looked thinner than usual, the bones in his face standing out. He'd grown a lot this past winter. Kelsey was always hungry. As hungry as Claire was.

A rustle of leaves brought Claire's gaze back to the forest. She strained to see through the bushes. In front of her was a moving red-brown shape. Maybe it was a deer. No, it was two deer. She could just see the moving shapes through the leaves.

Claire lowered her bow and arrow, and turned to Kelsey. He still had his arrow aimed at the deer.

"What are you doing?" she asked and grabbed his arm. "Has the hunger made you lose your mind? You know only King Rudgerd's men can kill deer."

Kelsey shook her hand away. "The King's men aren't here," he said. "And everyone in the village is hungry. A deer would feed many families."

The first deer poked its head through the bushes to stare at Claire and Kelsey. Its big liquid eyes were intelligent and wary. Then the deer cocked its head to one side, its ears flicking. It seemed to wonder what Kelsey was going to do.

"Kelsey!" Claire caught his arm again. She saw something in the look of the deer that wasn't animal, but wasn't fully human, either. "Stop! It's not a deer. It's a Skinwalker!"

"All the more reason to kill it," Kelsey said.

He sent his arrow flying.

"No!" Claire cried, grabbing at his arm. But it was too late.

The arrow shot through the air, straight at the deer. The arrow caught the animal right in its throat. Blood spurted, spraying on the leaves. The deer staggered, then fell to its knees.

Claire ran forward. "No!" Dread filled her. *Don't let it be a Skinwalker*, she thought.

When she pushed aside the bushes, she saw the deer lying limply on its side. Blood was pooling into the earth and staining the deer's coat. Its chest was still — it would never breathe again.

But this was not a deer, not an ordinary deer. As Claire watched, the dead deer began to change form. Its nose and muzzle shrank, pulling inward. Its neck shortened; its torso lengthened. Fur pulled back to reveal pale white skin. Soon a young man lay in front of them, an arrow through his throat.

Claire knelt beside the Skinwalker. "I'm sorry," she whispered. "I'm so sorry."

She looked over her shoulder at Kelsey. Her cousin stood still. He didn't come over to see if he'd killed a deer or a Skinwalker. Maybe he already knew.

The other deer, still watching from a few paces back, turned and leaped away from them. It ran deeper into the forest, its white tail bobbing an alert.

Claire looked back angrily at her cousin. *Nothing good would come of this.*

Kelsey slowly came forward to look at the dead animal. Claire turned around, her heart heavy. "You shot a Skinwalker."

Kelsey grinned, holding his bow up to the sky. "Good riddance! We're better off without another of those monsters around."

"They're not monsters. *We're* not. . . ."

Kelsey turned his head away. "You saw what the villagers did to my mother and yours," he said. "They were keeping us safe. Why else would they kill them? Now help me carry this thing back to the village. The people will want to celebrate."

Claire stared at Kelsey in horror. Her cousin could be thoughtful and brave, but right now she didn't know him at all.

"You just killed someone, Kelsey."

"Not someone. Some *thing*. If we can't eat it, we may as well get the reward."

"I'm not going to help you do that," Claire replied. "This Skinwalker — he'll have people who will want to grieve. They'll want their own burial."

"They're monsters, Claire," Kelsey spat out. "Stop giving them feelings where they have none."

Claire turned away from him. "I won't help you," she said again. "You should leave the body here. Let his people collect him."

"Do you really think they would do the same for us?" Kelsey yelled.

Claire walked away without replying.

"Claire! Claire, get back here."

But Claire kept walking. She couldn't believe her cousin could be so unfeeling. He didn't care that he had killed another being — and not for food. He hadn't been like this before. Before his mother was murdered. Before the village kids had begun to bully him. Now he was just like the others.

"Claire, come on!" Kelsey shouted.

Claire ignored him. She didn't want to return to her grandfather with empty hands. He would never admit it, but she knew he was hungry too. Claire still had to find something her family could eat.

Claire strode deeper into the forest, away from Kelsey and his kill. She walked silently, the way she had trained herself to. There was a trick to it — putting each foot down slowly, avoiding dried twigs and branches.

Forest sounds started up again — birds calling to each other, insects buzzing. Claire heard a scurrying sound in the bushes, then saw a flash of white-brown fur. She watched carefully. A rabbit was rooting around for food, not yet aware of her. She couldn't see any sign of human intelligence in its eyes. This wasn't a Skinwalker.

Claire's arrow killed the rabbit instantly. Then she picked up the rabbit, tied its feet with cord and pulled out her arrow to use again. She slung the rabbit over her shoulder. At least they'd have a meal tonight. It would be a little bit more than the berries she'd managed to find.

Far behind her, she heard whoops and shouts. Kelsey must be showing off his kill to the men of the village. The same men who had killed her mother . . . and his. Claire started back toward home, wishing she could avoid them all.

As Claire approached the village, she heard singing. She saw women coming out of their houses with what little food they could spare. Men threw down their tools and shouted with joy. The whole village seemed to be celebrating the death of the Skinwalker.

"Claire — the Skinwalker Killer!" a boy shouted.

Claire halted in surprise. Usually, none of the villagers spoke to her, not unless they were mocking her for having Skinwalker blood. But now they thought she'd taken part in the killing. Claire shuddered and started walking again.

More and more people shouted out to her, but she pretended she didn't hear them. Claire walked faster toward her grandfather's house.

Claire's grandfather waited in the doorway, his eyes full of shadows. "Kelsey killed one, didn't he?" he asked.

Claire nodded, her eyes stinging.

"There goes another piece of magic from our world," the old man said. He looked so sad and weary, Claire wanted to weep.

CHAPTER TWO | Arrested

The villagers' party went on into the late afternoon. The men kept getting louder as the ale went to their heads.

Claire and her grandfather stayed in their house, trying to ignore the sounds. But her grandfather shook his head and sighed. He kept busy carving shapes from the soft wood he always had on hand. Claire couldn't block out the rowdy laughter coming from the square, no matter how hard she tried to think of something else.

Claire cleaned her arrow and put it away. Then she gutted the rabbit and hung up the fur to dry.

By then, the noise from the village had dropped off. Claire's grandfather set his carving down with trembling hands. Claire knew he was thinking about the villagers who had killed the women he loved. He'd been away, trading his carvings in another village. When he had returned, it was all too late.

Now the memories haunted him. Sometimes he woke in the middle of the night, crying out their names. Claire would run to him and hold his hand.

Claire had nightmares herself. It had only been three years since the killings. But Claire didn't scream aloud when she dreamed. Her screams never made it out of her throat. The terrible memories stayed inside her.

Claire went to her grandfather and rested her hand on his shoulder. The old man looked up at her, smiling through his tears. Claire smiled back. She'd always loved her grandfather, but now he was the only family she had left. Except for her cousin, Kelsey, and after today Claire didn't want to see him again.

Hoof beats sounded in the distance. Claire went to the doorway to look out.

It was the King's soldiers passing through the village. The earth trembled beneath the horses' hooves as they

rode into the village square. The villagers should have bowed, or at the least shown some respect, but they didn't even notice.

The lead soldier halted. The other six soldiers came to a stop behind him, drawing their horses up. The lead soldier leaned down to the crowd. "You're in a good mood," he called. "What are you celebrating?"

"A Skinwalker has been killed!" The villagers lifted

up mugs of ale to the soldiers.

The lead soldier dismounted. He smiled, drinking the ale. "I'd like to see this Skinwalker. Show me."

The crowd parted to reveal the dead boy, laid out in the middle of the clearing. His skin was pale, drained of blood.

The lead soldier bent down to look, turning the body over.

Claire dashed out of the house towards the crowd. She kept looking for Kelsey as she ran. She had to reach Kelsey before he said something stupid.

The soldier straightened up in his saddle. "Who killed this Skinwalker?" he asked.

"I did!" Kelsey said loudly. His chest was puffed out in pride.

"You and your cousin, more like!" someone cried from the crowd. They all knew Claire was a better shot than Kelsey. In fact, she was better than most of the village boys. The crowd laughed loudly, the ale making them more loose-tongued than usual.

Claire came up beside Kelsey. "Hush!"

"No, it was me!" Kelsey said loudly. "My aim is just as good as Claire's."

The lead soldier wiped his hands together. "From the eyes and the tail that's still attached, it looks like this

Skinwalker took the form of a deer."

"He sure did," Kelsey said. "Tricky old devil, too. Looked just like a regular deer."

"So you were hunting deer? The King's deer on the King's land," the lead soldier said.

Kelsey's face turned white. He finally understood what was happening. "No, I — well — Claire knew it was a Skinwalker. She tried to stop me," Kelsey said. He turned to Claire for help. "Isn't that right?"

"Yes," Claire said, loudly enough for the soldier to hear. "I knew it was a Skinwalker before he shot."

"But you shot it anyway," the soldier said sternly. He frowned at Kelsey. "You shot it in deer form."

"Yes, but — but — " Kelsey spluttered.

"Then you are under arrest for hunting the King's deer," the soldier said. Another guard tied Kelsey's wrists behind his back. He turned to Claire. "And you are, too, for helping him."

Before Claire could protest, a soldier jerked her arms behind her back. Soon her wrists were tied. The leather bit into her skin.

The crowd began to back away. People shook their heads, muttering under their breath. They knew not to oppose the soldiers. It would only get them arrested, too. Or worse.

"Let her go!" Kelsey shouted at them. "She didn't have anything to do with this. I'm the one who killed the deer. I'm the one you want."

"Sorry, son," the lead soldier said. "You were hunting together. And she didn't stop you. In the King's eyes, you're both guilty."

"What are you going to do to us?" Claire asked. Her voice wavered slightly. She cursed herself for showing that weakness.

The soldier looked down his nose at her and arched one eyebrow. "We'll take you back to the King's court, of course. The court will see to your punishment." He turned to the other soldiers, and motioned toward the dead Skinwalker. "Get this thing packed on my horse. We'll need it for evidence."

Two of the soldiers jumped down from their horses and heaved the body onto the back of the lead soldier's horse.

"Let's go!" the lead soldier shouted. One soldier picked up the long leather strap trailing from Claire's wrists. Another grabbed Kelsey's, and they started off. Claire and Kelsey walked behind, trying not to choke on the dust that the horses kicked up.

Claire looked back over her shoulder trying to find her grandfather, but she couldn't see him. Claire's chest ached. One of the villagers would tell him what had happened. But there was nothing the old man could do. There was nothing that could save Claire and Kelsey from the King's rough justice.

CHAPTER THREE | Ambush

They were barely out of the village when Kelsey spoke up. "You shouldn't arrest us for killing a Skinwalker. You should give us a reward!"

"Aye, you're right!" the lead soldier called back. He took a swallow of the villager's ale. The six other soldiers all did the same.

Claire stumbled, the leather strap around her wrists pulling tight. She wished Kelsey would shut up. It was useless to talk to the soldiers.

"Then what are you doing, arresting us?" Kelsey asked.

"It's the law, my boy. It's the law," the lead soldier said. He turned in his saddle to look at Kelsey. "We can't have anyone stealing the King's deer, can we? But when he hears you killed a Skinwalker, he's sure to forgive you. And he might even reward you. You never know." He slapped the dead Skinwalker tied to the back of his horse. The other soldiers laughed.

Claire shuddered. *These* men were the monsters. Not the innocent Skinwalker that Kelsey had killed.

Kelsey glanced over at Claire. "I'm sorry I got us into this, Claire," he said. "I wasn't thinking."

"We'll be okay," Claire told him. But she wasn't sure about that. The King wasn't very forgiving. His soldiers were often brutal long before their prisoners reached the courts.

"I did it to protect us," Kelsey said.

"Protect us? The Skinwalker wasn't threatening us."

"Yes, he was. Standing there looking at us, knowing all about us. Knowing that we're part Skinwalker — that's what got our family killed."

Claire shook her head. Kelsey never talked about the murders. He never even said their mothers' names. He just walked away when anyone else talked about them. It was as if he wanted to bury the memory, to deny what happened. Yet here he was, bringing it up himself.

Claire frowned, trying to understand. "It's human hatred that killed our family. And fear. The Skinwalkers aren't the ones who threaten us."

"Skinwalkers threaten us all," Kelsey said.

"I can't believe you're repeating what the villagers say. Don't you have a mind of your own?" Claire cried. "Don't you remember how wonderful they all were? Grandmother . . . your mother . . . mine. How much they loved us."

One of the soldiers turned around. "If you talk like this in the dungeons, things will go badly for you."

Claire wasn't sure if he meant that or not. "We're talking about our family!" she shot back.

The soldier laughed. "Just a warning," he repeated.

Kelsey turned away from her, but she knew their talk was over. Kelsey moved up ahead of her and started talking to the soldiers, instead. Claire hung back. She felt sad and upset — with Kelsey, the soldiers, and everything.

The deeper they got into the woods, the more uncomfortable Claire felt. It seemed as if someone was watching them.

Kelsey and the soldiers were unaware, talking loudly. The soldiers kept drinking more and more, but Claire's skin crawled. Claire was a good hunter. She knew what

it felt like to stalk prey. Only now, they were the ones being stalked. She was sure of it.

"Kelsey!" she hissed.

Kelsey shrugged his shoulders.

"Kelsey! We're being watched!" Claire said louder.

Kelsey looked over at her this time. "Watched by who? Skinwalkers?"

Claire nodded her head. "I think so."

Kelsey looked over his shoulder. Then he fell silent. Even the soldiers got quieter, as if they felt Claire's fear. They put away their ale and sat up straighter in their saddles. Some put their hands on the hilts of their swords. They pushed their horses to trot at a faster pace. Kelsey and Claire almost had to run to keep up.

The forest was eerily quiet now. There were no birdsongs, no chattering squirrels. The soldiers kept looking all around them, peering into the shadows. But the shadows revealed nothing.

Then a twig snapped. Bushes rustled. In seconds, wolves and deer burst through the bushes to surround them.

Claire's breath caught in her throat. Wolves and deer working together. They had to be Skinwalkers.

The wolves growled deep in their throats, teeth bared, yellow eyes glowing. Their fur stood up in ridges on their necks. The deer snorted and pawed at the ground. Their nostrils flared as if they might attack. There were at least twenty Skinwalkers. Claire, Kelsey, and the soldiers were badly outnumbered.

Claire's mouth went dry. The soldiers drew their swords as the Skinwalkers formed a circle around him.

"Away with you!" the lead soldier shouted. His horse whinnied nervously, shying away from the wolves.

The largest wolf rose on his hind legs. The silver in his dark coat suggested that he was older. Suddenly his head changed to a man's. A stern, handsome man with bright, hard eyes. "Give us our dead," the man said. His voice was deep and cold.

The lead soldier spat, then swung his sword in an arc toward the wolf.

The Skinwalker howled, his face turning back into a wolf's. He leapt at the soldier's throat, tearing into the man's skin.

The soldier gave a gurgling cry as his blood spurted out. The blood was like a signal. Soon all the other wolves and deer had launched themselves at the soldiers.

The soldier holding Claire's leather strap dropped it. He reached for his sword just as a wolf tore at his shoulder. Soon his skin had ripped open to reveal pink muscle and blood.

Claire backed away, feeling sick. She crouched down, then stepped back through her bound arms, bringing them up in front of her. She looked around, wildly. The soldier's sword lay on the ground. Claire turned the sword so that the sharp length of the blade rose toward her. She held the sword steady between her feet. Then she pushed her bound wrists against the edge of the blade. She rubbed the leather back and forth until the sword sliced through it. Then Claire leapt up, grabbing the heavy sword with both hands.

"Get me out of this!" Kelsey cried.

Claire slashed at his straps, and the leather fell away. Kelsey picked up a fallen dagger, and the two of them stood back to back. They were ready to fight off the wolves and deer if they had to.

Around them were soldiers on the ground, groaning from their wounds or lying still in pools of blood. A few were still fighting it out with the Skinwalkers. Now both sides had bleeding wounds.

As Claire watched, a deer Skinwalker changed her hoof to a human hand. The hand removed a horse's reigns. Then it slapped the back of the sweating horse, and the deer cried out in a language Claire couldn't understand. The horse ran away through the bush, safe from the fighting.

Claire looked around her. The fighting was slowing down, with only two soldiers left standing. The Skinwalkers were beginning to turn to her and Kelsey. Surrounding them. The yellow eyes of the wolves frightened her the most.

Claire's hands tightened on the sword. "Please — we didn't mean to kill one of your kind!" she cried.

The lead wolf growled low in his throat. His body was crouched, ready to jump.

A deer near Claire transformed his face into human-like features. His curly red-brown hair matched the color of his deer coat. "She tells the truth, brothers and sisters," the deer/man said. "She tried to stop the boy from killing him. I was there. I saw it."

The big, silver-haired wolf growled, then changed his head to a man's again. "Then we will spare her life, out of respect for what she's done."

Claire clasped her hands together. "Thank you!"

"Don't talk to them, Claire — they're not even human," Kelsey said.

The wolves growled deep in their throats. The deer snorted and pawed at the ground. Claire almost wished a wolf Skinwalker would bite Kelsey, just to shut him up. He was only making things worse.

"But the boy will go on trial for killing one of us." The wolves crowded around Kelsey, growling low in their throats. "You," the wolf leader said, nodding at Claire, "can come along as our guest."

Claire raised her head higher, trying not to look afraid. "Am I free to leave, then?" she asked. "If I'm your guest?"

"No." The wolf Skinwalker shook his head. "You will

remain as our guest, and will be treated as such. Later the tribe will decide your fate."

A deer Skinwalker changed her front legs into human hands and arms. Using these, she tied Kelsey's wrists with cord woven from plants. She looked at Claire and nodded, leaving Claire's wrists unbound.

Two deer Skinwalkers untied the dead Skinwalker from the horse. Gently they carried the body between them. Then they all set off in a group. The wolves guarded Kelsey, sometimes nipping at his heels. The deer looked after Claire.

All of them walked deeper into the woods, away from the village, away from Claire's home. Soon they'd be far away from everything Claire knew.

CHAPTER FOUR | More Revenge

The trees grew closer together, and branches slapped at Claire's face. Claire's feet ached from walking. The village was far behind them now. She'd paid attention to the direction they'd walked. Her memory might be their only way to get back.

"You're not human, any of you!" Kelsey cried to the Skinwalkers. "I'm not sorry that I killed one of you. A man needs to hunt — for food and to keep his family safe. I'd kill you all if I had the chance."

The wolves growled again, showing their teeth. One

of them tore at Kelsey's tunic, sharp teeth scraping at his flesh.

The old wolf was mostly in human form. He spoke quietly. "If humans had captured you, you'd already be dead. But we, at least, care about *all* life."

"You're not human enough to care!"

"Kelsey, shut up!" Claire said. She knew he was trying to act confident. But couldn't he see that he was only stirring up bad feeling? He was giving a bad name to humans. "We're at their mercy," she said. Maybe that would make sense to him.

Kelsey scowled at her. He looked like he had more to say, but then he went quiet.

The group walked in silence — the wolves, the deer, and Kelsey and Claire. Without Kelsey challenging the Skinwalkers, the tension eased. Claire's racing heart slowed down. Kelsey and Claire were still prisoners — but they hadn't been hurt. Not yet.

Suddenly the wolf and deer Skinwalkers all stopped at once. Claire looked around her. She couldn't see any reason for the sudden halt. It was just another part of the forest.

"This is where we will have to leave you, brothers and sisters," the wolf leader said to the deer. He turned his human head to glare at Kelsey. "If these humans give you any problems, call us."

"We will. And thank you for your help," the deer Skinwalker leader replied.

"Treat them as they deserve," said the wolf. "One of them is no friend of ours."

The wolves disappeared into the woods. Soon they blended into the forest until Claire couldn't see them anymore.

Still, the group did not move on. Claire looked around her warily. There had to be a reason they'd stopped here. She peered into the trees and bushes, squinting, trying to see what was different. And then she saw something. There was a small hut made of branches and leaves. The roof looked just like branches stretching out from the tree, covered with leaves. The sides looked like part of the trunk of one tree and part of the brush on the other side. Claire could barely see that it was a hut — and she was good at seeing what was in front of her.

Claire caught a slight movement, and stared harder. Had she been blind? There wasn't just one hut — there were at least eight of them, scattered throughout the trees.

"I see you've spotted our village," the deer Skinwalker leader said. She transformed her deer head to a woman's face. "Don't think you can bring your human warriors back here. We move camp all the time."

"I would never!" Claire said.

Kelsey started to say something. Claire bumped into him hard, startling him into silence.

The deer Skinwalkers shoved Kelsey forward. Claire started to follow her cousin.

The deer Skinwalker leader held up her forearm. "We are taking the boy to the holding area, where he will await trial. You will have a separate hut."

Claire watched as the deer pushed Kelsey into a small hut.

It made sense, when she thought about it. The deer Skinwalkers didn't want Kelsey and her to talk. They couldn't risk Claire and Kelsey finding a way to reveal their camp.

Claire couldn't blame them, after all the stupid things Kelsey had said. Why did he have to attack the very group that had saved them from the King's guards?

"Fine," Claire said. It wasn't like she had a choice. Still, she watched to see where they were taking Kelsey.

The Skinwalker leader turned to the deer who had spoken for Claire earlier. "Ned, do you want to take care of our guest?"

Ned transformed his deer head to a human one. "Sure." His eyes were big and gentle, his face soft. He

looked only a year or two older than Claire. "Follow me, please," he said.

Claire followed him into the village. Young Skinwalkers — some in deer shape, some in human shape, some taking both — came out to stare when they saw Claire. She wondered how they knew she was human and not Skinwalker. "How do they know I'm not one of you?" she asked.

Ned looked at her with laughing eyes. "It's your scent."

"My scent?" Claire said, her nose wrinkling. Did she smell bad?

"Yes, your scent." Ned nodded. "You smell human. It's a very strong, distinct smell. And then you — " He turned his head toward her, his nose turning into a deer's. "You also smell like pine and bread and . . . " His nostrils flared. "Like roses."

Claire flushed. She had used rose water to wash her hair. Grandfather had traded one of his wood carvings for the mixture for her. It was a gift for her birthday that she tried to use sparingly.

Grandfather, she thought. Suddenly her chest felt hollow. Who would hunt for him now and make sure he was fed? Who would listen to his old stories and ask him for more? Who would bring happiness to his eyes with a smile?

Ned stopped walking. "Are you all right?"

"Of course." Claire brushed at her eyes. "I just miss my family. And I'm worried about Kelsey."

They started walking into the camp. Young Skinwalkers poked their heads out from behind their mothers, then hid again. One young Skinwalker bravely trotted up to them. He turned his hoof to a hand, poked one finger at Claire, then raced back again.

Ned shook his head. "Children." He looked at Claire. "Why do you care about that boy, Kelsey? He seems so full of anger and hatred. Not like you." That last was said softly, almost shyly.

"Kelsey's my cousin. My only family except for my grandfather," Claire said. She felt the need to explain — to make Ned see that Kelsey wasn't as bad as he seemed. "Our grandmother was half Skinwalker. Our mothers were a quarter. The villagers — they made it tough for Kelsey and me growing up. They called us Skinwalkers and said we weren't even human. Kelsey had to fight them or become like them. If Kelsey's mean, it's because he's had to be."

"But you're not," Ned said.

"No," Claire said slowly. "I'm not." She shrugged. She didn't know how to explain it, but she could never hate anyone, not the way the villagers did. She knew the suffering that hatred caused. "My grandmother, my mother — they were good people. Loving people."

"What happened to them?"

Claire looked away, her eyes clouding. "They were killed." *By the villagers* — but she didn't dare say that to Ned.

There was a silence. Claire felt Ned react. She looked back at him.

"Because they were part Skinwalker?" he said. "Your villagers killed them for that?"

"Yes," Claire said miserably.

"Could they change?" Ned asked.

"My grandmother could. My mother and aunt could change only if they really focused. Sometimes she just had to, my mother told me. To feel right. But Kelsey and I . . . we can't. That's why . . ." Claire's breath hitched. "That's why we were spared." It hurt to say it. But it felt good, too — like a release. Like Claire was sharing her guilt, making it lighter.

Ned stopped, clasped Claire's hand in his warm ones. "I'm sorry. That must have been very hard."

Claire nodded, tears pricking her eyes.

Ned cleared his throat. "We're here."

Claire blinked. They were standing outside a leafy hut, built like a lean-to. It was big enough for two, maybe three, people to sit side by side. There was a bowl of water tucked in one corner, and an empty bowl beside it. Soft moss layered the ground. A woven, knotted cord necklace hung on the wall.

"It looks like somebody's home," Claire said.

"It is a home. It's mine. You will share it with me until Kelsey goes to trial."

"Oh." Claire was surprised. She didn't know what she'd expected, but this wasn't it.

"I've just moved into my own dwelling," Ned said. "It will be empty until I find myself a mate."

Claire stepped backward, though she didn't know why. A Skinwalker wouldn't want to be with a human. How could they? But Skinwalkers could take human form . . . .

"When can I see my cousin?" Claire asked. She was trying to cover up her reaction.

Ned looked up at the darkening sky. "Tomorrow. It's getting late now."

What did the time have to do with seeing Kelsey? It would take only a minute to walk over to the hut where Kelsey was being kept. Still, Claire didn't want to upset the Skinwalkers — not until she had to.

"There's water to drink," Ned went on. "One of the children will fetch you berries and some wild lettuce if you're hungry."

Claire pushed her hair out of her eyes. "Thank you." She *was* hungry. Fiercely so.

"We don't eat meat," Ned replied. "It is not in our nature. But we know that humans do. If you really want meat, I will ask our wolf brothers and sisters to bring you some."

Claire thought of the wolf Skinwalkers and shuddered. "No. This is good. Berries will be enough."

Ned nodded, then called out in a strange language. A young deer Skinwalker scampered up to them, carrying a bunched cloth in his mouth. He tipped the cloth into the empty bowl. Wild strawberries, blackberries, and blueberries tumbled out. The young Skinwalker looked at Claire out of the corners of his eyes, stamping nervously on the hard ground.

"Thank you," Claire said.

The young deer snorted, then trotted away.

"Your supper," Ned said. "If you need anything else, let me know. We treat our guests well."

Unlike humans, Claire knew he wanted to add. She thought of the stakes in the middle of her village. The stakes were used to burn Skinwalkers to death. The villagers would burn Skinwalkers and anyone suspected of being a Skinwalker.

But here it was different. The deer Skinwalkers were being more human than the humans in Claire's village. How was it possible?

Claire's stomach rumbled and clenched. She chewed the berries, feeling their juicy sweetness burst through her mouth. She swallowed, wishing she had more. Then she licked the juice off her fingers. She wondered if Kelsey had gotten food. She wondered how he was being treated. Surely they wouldn't kill him?

"If you can, you should sleep," Ned told her. "It will make tomorrow come sooner."

Claire smiled to herself. That's what her grandfather always told her. She lay back and closed her eyes. A song drifted through the forest — soft and lilting. It sounded like the leaves rustling on the trees.

The music wrapped around Claire like a blanket. Tears spilled from her eyes. Her grandmother used to sing her that song when Claire couldn't sleep. There were no words — at least no words that Claire understood — but somehow the sounds caught the peacefulness of the forest.

Ned looked down at her from where he was sitting. "What is it?" he asked.

"That song — do you know it?"

Ned tilted his head to listen. He smiled. "Yes. Every

deer mother sings it to her child."

"Will you teach it to me?" Claire asked.

Ned looked at her, puzzled.

"My grandmother used to sing it to me," Claire said, a catch in her voice. "I thought no one else knew it."

Ned touched her hand. "Of course I'll teach it to you."

He sang the first line, over and over, until Claire could repeat it back to him. The song helped ease her worry for Kelsey. It helped her forget the fighting and bloodshed of the day. It made her think that tomorrow, somehow, the world would be a better place.

CHAPTER FIVE | Curious

The morning sun shone on Claire's face. The light made red and orange squiggles behind her eyelids. The songs of birds were loud and cheerful. Claire stretched and opened her eyes to see dozens of faces — children's and young deer — surrounding her.

"Ahh!" Claire screamed, sitting bolt upright.

The young Skinwalkers screamed, too. They leapt away and ran in all directions.

Ned was in the hut, watching all this. He laughed. "The young ones scared you?" he asked. "They're just curious, Claire. They've never been this close to a real human before."

Claire glared at Ned. "You'd be scared, too, if you woke up to a bunch of strangers that close to your face."

Ned raised one eyebrow, and snorted. "I'd say you scared them and they scared you. It was pretty even."

Claire found it hard to look away from Ned's handsome, open face. She liked the way his lips curved easily into a smile. And she liked how soft his springy red-brown curls looked.

Claire ran her fingers through her own messy hair. She shook out some twigs and bits of moss. She heard footsteps, then looked at the door of the hut.

The young ones were coming back, peering at her. Claire smiled at them. One darted forward, then shyly gave her some berries in a small square of cloth.

One young Skinwalker was braver than the others. "Is it true that you're stuck in one body?" she asked loudly. "That you can't ever take the shape of your animal?"

The other young Skinwalkers giggled.

"It's true," Claire replied. Though she'd never really thought of it like that before.

The young Skinwalker stepped closer. "And do you eat meat, like our wolf brothers?"

Claire nodded. "We eat squirrels, birds, rabbits . . . ."

"Deer?" the young Skinwalker asked, fear in her eyes.

"Not deer," Claire said quickly. But she didn't explain that the King claimed all the deer as his. Only the King was allowed to eat deer.

The young Skinwalker pawed at the ground nervously. She looked like she wanted to run away.

"We would never eat a Skinwalker," Claire told her. "And I would never kill one."

The young Skinwalker just tilted her head, studying Claire. "I thought humans couldn't tell us apart."

"I can," Claire said. "I can see it in the way you move. You're more human-like than regular deer."

"We're not like humans at all!" the young Skinwalker protested. "You take that back!"

Claire tried not to laugh. The Skinwalker sounded almost like Kelsey.

"I'm sorry. You're not like humans. I didn't mean to offend you. You move much more gracefully than us. It's just — there's a difference. A knowledge that I don't see in . . . just deer."

"In One-Skins," the young Skinwalker said.

"Yes. In One-Skins." Claire found it strange to use that word. If she was a One-Skin, were they two-skins?

A voice called out. The young Skinwalker waved to

Claire, then trotted to her waiting parents. Claire sat back, feeling pleased with the morning talk. She was actually making friends with some of the Skinwalkers.

Claire's stomach rumbled. She felt even hungrier than the day before. A handful of berries wasn't enough. Maybe they had some cereal grains or even bread. No, that wasn't likely. It wasn't what deer ate.

A scream broke into Claire's thoughts. Kelsey! It was Kelsey's voice.

Claire leapt up but Ned blocked her way.

"Let me by!" Claire demanded.

Ned didn't move.

Kelsey screamed again, his voice muffled in the dense forest.

Claire dashed to the side, trying to get around Ned, but he blocked her again. Then Ned changed to his human form. He spread out his broad arms to stop her.

"Your cousin is not being hurt." Ned told her. "We don't do that here."

"Then why is he screaming?"

Ned shrugged his broad shoulders. "He does have a temper, you know."

Claire didn't dare look below Ned's face. She felt embarrassed to be with him.

Ned reached up and pulled a length of fabric down

from a branch, then wrapped it around his waist. "Better?" he said, grinning at her.

Claire felt her face grow hot. "I want to see my cousin. *Now*."

"You're not supposed to — "

"Why not? I'm not going to try to escape. I promise. I just want to make sure he's not hurt."

"And you're not going to give up until you see him, are you?" Ned said. "Fine. Walk with me."

Claire walked beside Ned through the forest. Claire knew Ned was her guard. If she had to be guarded by anyone, she was glad it was him.

As they got closer to the screaming, Claire could make out some of what Kelsey was saying: "You filthy, murdering monsters! You won't get away with this, let me tell you! You're the dead ones, not me."

Claire walked faster, Ned close beside her.

They neared a hut where a deer Skinwalker stood. She had all four legs placed firmly apart, her back to the door opening. Her ears were flat against her head, as if that could help block out Kelsey's screams.

Kelsey stood inside the hut, his wrists bound with sturdy vines. His face was red from yelling. A bowl lay on its side at his feet, berries and nuts scattered all around.

The Skinwalker grew stiff and formal as Claire and Ned approached. "Turn around and walk away," she told Claire. "You're not welcome here."

Kelsey jerked his head up. "Claire! Run if you can! They're trying to kill us."

Claire's chest tightened. She looked at Kelsey's guard, then at Ned, searching for signs that they wanted to hurt her. No. She didn't think they had it in them. There wasn't violence in their eyes, like there was in the wolves' eyes. Or in the eyes of some of the villagers. There was anger, but not violence.

"They're monsters, Claire. You know that! Run!" Kelsey yelled. He turned to look at his guard. "Just wait until my people get hold of you. You'll be dead before you know it!"

Shame washed over Claire. She could only hope the Skinwalkers didn't think all humans were like this.

"Let me talk to him a little," Claire said to the guard. "Maybe I can calm him down."

Ned and the angry guard looked at each other and shrugged. Kelsey's guard nodded slowly. "The noise is upsetting the young ones. But we'll be standing right here, so don't think you can try anything."

"I won't."

The guard stepped aside. Claire entered the hut, and

knelt by Kelsey.

"What are you doing? Get out of here!" Kelsey said.

Claire shook her head. "The deer Skinwalkers — they're a peaceful people. Can't you feel it?"

"They tried to poison me with those purple berries!" Kelsey said. He pointed at the berries on the ground.

Claire looked at the berries. "Poison you with blackberries and blueberries? They gave me some last night. And look at me. I'm fine." She couldn't believe Kelsey was wasting good food — not when it was so hard to find. Claire reached down and picked up a berry and popped it into her mouth. "If you're not going to eat them, I will."

"Claire!" Kelsey grabbed her wrist. "Spit it out!"

"I told you — the berries are safe," Claire said, swallowing. "The Skinwalkers are not trying to hurt you, Kelsey. They're giving us their own food."

The two guards were watching them — Kelsey's guard suspiciously, Claire's guard with interest.

Claire hunched closer to Kelsey. "What are you doing, yelling threats at them? Are you trying to get them to hurt you? Stop calling them names. They're good people, Kelsey."

"They're not people. I don't care if they can look like us. They're not human."

"So, your mother and my mother and Grandmother were not human?" Claire asked.

Kelsey scowled. "I'm just trying to get us out of here, Claire. You'll see. Someone will hear me sooner or later. Our people won't leave us here."

"So that's why you're yelling." Claire sat back on her heels. "If you're only yelling to be heard, can you stop calling them names? Why make them angry?"

Kelsey spat on the ground. "You're seeing them as people, Claire. They're not."

"I think you're being stupid. You're insulting them, saying things that would make anyone angry. I'm surprised they haven't done anything to keep you quiet. Please, Kelsey — for me — stop yelling!"

Kelsey looked skyward. "For you."

"Enough talk now," Kelsey's guard said, looking in at them. "You're not even supposed to be here."

Claire rose.

"Be careful, Claire!" Kelsey said, catching at her hand.

"You be careful, too," Claire said sadly. She knew they meant very different things.

Claire walked back to the hut with Ned in silence.

"We would never hurt him, you know," Ned said. "Unless he attacks us, we will let him be."

Ned had been listening, though he'd pretended not to. Claire wagged her finger at him, half smiling.

Ned flushed. "We have good hearing," he said. He transformed his ears to deer ears, then back again. "I couldn't help it."

Kelsey started screaming again.

Claire sighed. She thought Ned deserved to know why. "He's trying to tell the villagers where we are, to get them to rescue us," Claire said.

Ned nodded. "What do you suggest we do? Gag him?"

The villagers would. They'd do a lot worse than that, Claire thought.

"We're a peaceful people, Claire. Deer Skinwalkers believe in freedom — unless lives are threatened."

"And then you'll fight?" Claire asked, her stomach tightening.

"If we have to."

Claire bit her lip. She thought Kelsey was probably right — the villagers would be out looking for them. Especially since Skinwalkers were involved. "I don't think we should stay here. The villagers are going to come."

"Then they will come," Ned said, shrugging. "We have no quarrel with them — only with your cousin. It was your cousin who killed one of us."

"But the villagers won't think that way. They'll want to kill all of you."

"Why?" Ned asked, sounding confused.

"You killed those soldiers."

"We only wanted back the body of one of our own. The soldiers were going to kill us. What else could we do?"

Claire gritted her teeth. The deer Skinwalkers — they lived by a different code. A kinder one. They were never going to understand how humans thought.

Claire sat uneasily through the noon meal. She talked to the young ones when they came to stare at her. Then she paced around the small hut. Kelsey's trial would be the next day. Until then, there was nothing she could do but wait.

By the time the late afternoon shadows crept in, Claire and Ned were sitting outside the hut. They were sharing berries and nuts, talking about what might happen at the trial.

Then Ned heard something. He transformed his ears into those of a deer and listened to the forest.

Soon Claire could hear the sounds, too. Twigs snapped in the quiet forest. Bushes rustled, more twigs and branches cracked. Something was moving through the woods.

Ned's head snapped up. "Stay here," he said, leaping to his feet.

Ned beat a rhythm on the ground with his hooves. The young ones scattered away just as hoarse cries came blaring from the forest.

The villagers were here.

CHAPTER SIX | A Battle

Suddenly the villagers came pouring into the Skinwalker camp.

They came with clubs, lances and war hammers. They ran into the village, screaming like madmen, smashing at the Skinwalker huts.

"Stop!" Claire cried. "Stop! We've been treated well."

But the villagers didn't listen. They went from hut to hut, pulling out the young ones hiding inside. Then one of the villagers came with a torch, and soon a hut was up in flames.

Only then did the Skinwalkers fight back. There was no way they could talk to these One-Skins. Now they had to protect their young ones . . . and themselves.

Soon it was a battle. Skinwalkers used their deer hooves to kick and their teeth to bite. Some transformed their legs to human arms to swing branches and throw rocks.

But the villagers had bows and arrows, knives, clubs, and pitchforks. The villagers kept attacking without stopping.

All around her, Claire heard screams and cries. She heard the thud of clubs and hooves against flesh. She smelled fear and blood in the air.

Claire scanned the villagers, looking for her grandfather, but he wasn't there. Then she caught sight of Hab, the village leader. It was Hab's father who had killed Claire's mother, aunt, and grandmother. But Hab was a gentler man now. Perhaps he'd listen to reason.

"Hab!" she called out to him.

"Claire!" Hab swung her way, striking at deer hooves with his staff.

Ned charged toward them.

Ned and Hab stared at each other, their eyes angry, their bodies tense. Ned's deer back rippled, his ears flattened.

Claire pushed her way between them. "I know neither of you want to hurt me," she said. "So don't go hurting each other."

"We've come to take you and your cousin back to the village," Hab told her.

"Is that why you're burning their huts?" Claire snapped back. "Is that your idea of a rescue?"

An arrow whistled by Hab's shoulder, narrowly missing him. Hab spun around, shaking his fist. "Watch where you're aiming, you numbskull!" Hab turned back and reached for Claire's arm. "Come with me, now. We'll get you home safe, away from these monsters."

Claire yanked her arm away. "I can't."

"You can't?" Hab stared at her.

An arrow flew at Ned. He reared up and blocked it with his hooves.

Claire shook her head. "Kelsey killed a Skinwalker. Someone has to stand trial for what he did," Claire said.

"What are you talking about?" Hab replied. "You're talking nonsense. Come on, now, lass — come home with me."

Claire shook her head. "No, I told you. I'm staying."

Ned frowned at her. "We do not expect you to take Kelsey's place."

"Exactly!" Hab said. He looked surprised to find himself agreeing with a Skinwalker.

Ned turned to Claire. "You are free to go home," he said, just as an arrow flew toward him. "As for your cousin — " Ned's words were cut off.

"Watch out!" Claire cried, trying to push Ned away from the arrow's path. But she wasn't fast enough. The arrow sunk deep into Ned's side.

Ned screamed. His hot blood spurted out, spraying Claire's face and arms.

Claire panicked. She knew that she had to do something, but what? She hadn't been able to save her mother or her grandmother, but perhaps she could save Ned.

Claire had to act quickly. She tore the arrow out of his side, then pressed down hard on the wound, trying to stop the flow of blood. But she wasn't strong enough.

"Hab," she cried. Claire could feel Ned's laboured breathing beneath her hands.

"Leave the monster," Hab told her. "Let's get out of this evil place."

Claire ignored his words. "Hab — press down here!" she said. "We've got to stop the bleeding."

Hab stared at her like she'd gone mad.

"Hab," Claire snapped, "do it!" She didn't care that she was ordering the village leader around. All she cared about was saving Ned. "Ned saved my life — now help me save his."

Hab was confused. Save a Skinwalker? Take orders from a teenage girl? But the creature below him was hurt, perhaps dying. Was he really a monster?

"I need your help," Claire begged. "Show me you're human enough to care."

Hab threw down his war hammer, then knelt beside Claire. He pressed his hands against Ned's heaving side.

"Press hard," she said, moving her hands away from

the wound.

Hab did, looking bewildered.

The fight raged all around them. Rocks and arrows were flying, clubs and hooves were hitting limbs, breaking bones, splitting skulls. Everywhere there was pain and anger.

But here there was just one fallen Skinwalker. Ned. A good and honest being.

Claire ran behind Ned's hut. She'd seen some yarrow growing in a patch of sunlight there. Quickly she tore up the healing plant and ran with it to Ned, ducking rocks and arrows.

Ned was groaning. He flailed at the ground like he was trying to stand up.

"Don't you move," Claire snapped. She shoved Hab's hands aside, and pressed the leaves and petals of the yarrow flower hard onto the deep wound. The plant stopped most of the blood — but more spilled up and around it.

Claire bit down on her lip. Ned's face looked pale. "Ned — can you change into human form?"

Ned nodded weakly.

Claire sucked in her breath. She was taking a chance. She didn't know if this would help Ned or make things worse. But Ned was going to bleed to death if he stayed like this.

"Then change. *Now*," she said harshly.

Ned closed his eyes. At first nothing happened. Then his chest shrunk, his limbs lengthened, his fur disappeared and a human boy, almost a man, lay there on the ground.

Claire lifted the yarrow, pressing a new piece on the open flesh. The bleeding had slowed, almost stopped. It was as if the wound had gotten smaller when Ned changed form.

Claire sat back on her heels, breathing out with relief. She tore a strip off the bottom of her tunic, and wrapped it around Ned, tying it tightly to keep the wound closed and the yarrow in place.

Hab looked shaken. He stood and backed up a step, then another. Then he crossed himself, as if he'd seen the Devil.

He looked up past Ned, and stiffened. His face grew pale.

Claire followed his gaze. A wolf, his teeth bared, stepped into the clearing. Another wolf, and then another appeared — all advancing toward the villagers. The villagers huddled together, Kelsey with them. They kept backing away from the wolves and the angry deer Skinwalkers.

"Claire!" Kelsey cried out to her. "Come on! You can

escape with us!"

Claire shook her head. "Go on without me! I'm staying here!"

"What?" Kelsey asked. The villagers were running now, retreating into the woods.

"I'm staying here."

Kelsey looked at her a long moment. But the wolves kept advancing, snarling, heads held low. Their bodies were tight, ready to attack.

"We'll come back for you!" Kelsey shouted. Then he turned and fled with the rest of the villagers.

CHAPTER SEVEN | Too Many Dead

Claire hoped Kelsey wouldn't do anything stupid. She'd tried to tell him she was staying at the Skinwalker camp by choice. She was free to go . . . but she had chosen to stay.

Claire sighed and looked around the clearing. Five villagers lay on the ground, dead. Claire recognized them all. Soon the villagers would send someone back to take away their dead. They would get a proper funeral.

There were seven dead Skinwalkers, too. Some of them kept most of their deer form, others turned more to human form as they died.

Blood stained the ground, darkening the leaves and moss. The coppery smell was strong in Claire's nose. She gagged, trying not to vomit.

So many were dead. And for what? The Skinwalkers wouldn't have harmed Kelsey. If they'd only talked it out . . . but men never wanted to do that. Men, One-Skins, wanted action. They wanted revenge. They wanted anything but peace.

Claire pulled her torn tunic tighter around herself.

The wolves turned and stalked toward Claire, growling. Many of the deer joined them, some of them limping. They made a ring around Claire and Ned.

"You. You did this." It was the old, silver-haired wolf. His voice was deep and gravelly. His harsh gaze never left Claire's face. "You brought the humans here to attack. You told them how to find the Deer Clan camp."

"I didn't!" Claire cried.

"Then how else did they find this place so quickly? Humans don't use their senses the way we do. They could never find a Skinwalker camp on their own."

Claire pressed her lips together. She would not blame Kelsey and his yelling.

"Leave her alone," Ned said, struggling to sit up. "I would have bled to death if it wasn't for her."

The wolf leader looked at the blood on Claire's hands. Then he stared at the makeshift bandage on Ned's side. He turned back to Claire. The wolf's yellow eyes bore into hers. "The One-Skin saved one of us — again? I don't trust her. What are you plotting, girl?"

The other Skinwalkers muttered and shifted uneasily.

"Nothing!" Claire replied. "Ned's been kind to me. Of course I tried to help him." She looked around at all the Skinwalkers pleadingly. "I don't want any of us to be enemies."

"But we are," the wolf said. "Your kind kills our kind. Your new king makes a sport of hunting Skinwalkers. He tells your people that we're monsters, devils."

"Not all of us believe that," Claire said.

The wolf snorted. "As long as your kind kills us, we will be enemies."

Ned sat up straighter, pressing his hand against his wound. "Back off, Ulric. Claire has proven herself to be on our side many times over."

Now Claire knew his name — Ulric, leader of the Wolf Clan.

Ulric's lips rose in·a snarl, revealing sharp, yellowed teeth. "Very well. But if the girl betrays you, it's on your head."

Ulric spun around, his paws kicking up dirt into

Claire's face. She wondered if he did it on purpose. The others scattered, as well.

Claire breathed easier.

Many of the deer Skinwalkers had changed into human form to gather the dead. They picked the fallen bodies up gently, and laid them down to look more at rest. They piled the humans separately, but with clear respect. Each human face was covered with a cloth.

"We will leave your dead for your people to take back," Ned said. "So they can mourn their own."

Claire swallowed hard. She knew the villagers would never treat a Skinwalker so well.

"Is there anything I can do to help?" Claire asked.

A passing Skinwalker snorted. "You can stay away from the dead, One-Skin. You've caused enough trouble."

Claire looked away from the bodies. She recognized the dead villagers — and she thought she recognized many of the dead Skinwalkers as well. So many people were going to miss their loved ones that night. Claire's throat ached with unshed tears.

Ned groaned again and slowly staggered upright. Claire caught his arm and helped him back to his hut.

"I'm all right!" he said, but he still leaned on her.

Claire helped him lower himself to the ground.

"You need to lie down and rest," Claire said. "You've

lost a lot of blood."

"I'm fine," Ned said again, but his face still looked pale. Claire could see the weariness in his eyes.

They sat in silence for a while. Clearly Ned was thinking about something. At last he put his question into words. "Why didn't you go with them?" he asked.

"I did what I thought was right," Claire said. But she knew there was more to it than that. She was drawn to Ned, and to his gentle way of life. Some part of her felt that she belonged with the Skinwalkers. Her mother and grandmother had been Skinwalkers. Claire felt more like a Skinwalker herself. These Skinwalkers led peaceful lives. The people of her village could be brutal and cruel.

"Time to move camp!" a Skinwalker called out.

The deer Skinwalkers, still in human form, began taking down their huts. They gathered their few belongings in cloth sacks.

Claire knew why they were moving. It was to keep the villagers from finding them again. To keep from being ambushed again. The Wolf Clan might not always be close enough to rescue them.

Claire helped Ned take down his hut, and pack his few bowls and his cloak. Ned hung his necklace around his neck. It was easy to carry that way. They worked quietly together. Claire felt more comfortable with him than she did with any of the village boys. They felt right together. Except, of course, that he could become a deer with just a thought.

Claire sensed a strange silence. She glanced up to see deer Skinwalkers, who'd been friendly before the villagers' attack, glaring at her. The remaining wolves stood with them, their eyes hard.

Claire lowered her head. It made sense — her kind had just attacked and killed their kind. And the wolves, she was sure, were adding to the deer Skinwalkers' mistrust.

It wasn't going to be easy, staying with them now. If Ned turned on her, it would be unbearable. Still, Claire had done what she thought was right. She had made the choice to stay behind. She wasn't going to back away from it now.

She wasn't even sure if she could.

A wolf Skinwalker crept over to Claire. The wolf's head was low, his ears flat against his skull. His tail was pointed straight out behind him.

"Did you enjoy watching our kind get killed?" he asked in a low, deep voice.

"No, of course not!" Claire replied.

"Really, One-Skin? How can we ever trust your kind now?"

Claire had no answer. She merely shook her head.

All around her, Skinwalkers looked at her with hard, mistrusting eyes. The wolf Skinwalker who'd spoken turned his back on her. The other Skinwalkers did the same. They began picking up their few belongings, and walking out of the clearing. Ned picked up his sack, the hut folded and sticking out of the top. He and Claire joined the rear of the line of Skinwalkers.

"It won't be like this forever," Ned told her. "They'll forget in a week or two."

Claire didn't think so, but she did her best to smile. Hatred, she knew, had a way of outlasting good sense.

CHAPTER EIGHT | Mistrust

The Skinwalkers didn't forget their grudge against Claire. Instead, their coldness and mistrust seemed to grow.

The young Skinwalkers stopped coming to Ned's hut to peek in at Claire. They stopped leaving her presents. The adult Skinwalkers kept their children firmly at their sides, giving Claire dark looks as they passed her. There was no more easy laughter, no more happy cries as the deer children played in the forest. Instead, they were quiet and solemn.

Everyone in the camp knew that Claire was taking Kelsey's place. She was putting herself on trial for the Skinwalker murder. They seemed to forget that she was doing it freely.

The Skinwalkers moved camp again, then again. Each time they ignored Claire's questions. Only Ned stood with her.

After they'd moved the camp a third time, the Skinwalker who'd guarded Kelsey came up to Claire. "You did this," she said loudly. Other Skinwalkers turned to look. "You plotted with that boy. You told the One-Skins where to find us."

"I didn't!" Claire cried. "You've only been kind to me. I would never betray that."

"Bah!" The Skinwalker turned her back on Claire and walked away.

Claire's eyes stung. She had *chosen* to be here. She'd *tried* to protect the Skinwalkers many times. It wasn't fair that they didn't trust her.

The days started passing slowly for Claire. She felt very alone. There was Ned, of course, but all the other Skinwalkers stayed away from her. They seemed heavier. Different.

Claire wasn't afraid of any of them — though perhaps she should have been. She was sad for them. But she

couldn't understand why they had changed so much. Surely they'd had others killed by villagers? By One-Skins?

"Yes, of course we have," Ned told her when she asked him.

"So what's different?"

"I'd been trying to convince them to trust humans," Ned said. "To make peace with them. We've met some One-Skins who are friendly. There used to be this old man who'd walk the woods. He'd leave gifts for us — a wood carving, a loaf of bread. Sometimes he'd look around, as if sensing we were there. He'd tell us that he was sorry for the way we'd been treated."

Grandfather! Claire thought.

"I told them that there were others like him," Ned went on. "I said, if we tried, we could reason with all of you. You're intelligent beings."

"Some of us are," Claire replied. She felt a sense of shame sweep through her.

"We hadn't been attacked for many moons. The others were starting to see it my way. Even the Wolf Clan. We were all starting to feel hope."

"But then Kelsey killed one of you," Claire said sadly. Ned nodded.

Claire sighed. She wished Kelsey could see what he'd done. But he probably wouldn't care.

Then Claire started getting a regular visitor — an unwelcome visitor. The Skinwalker who'd guarded Kelsey came by Ned's hut. At first she just yelled insults. Then she started spitting at Claire. Finally she peed right onto Claire's sleeping place.

That's enough, Claire thought.

The next day, Claire waited for the Skinwalker guard. She looked deep into the guard's angry eyes. Beneath the rage, she could see pain and guilt. Claire could see that the Skinwalker guard blamed herself for Kelsey's escape. She blamed herself for all the Skinwalkers who'd been killed that day.

"It wasn't your fault," Claire said quietly.

"What? How did you know? How — " A wail tore from the guard's throat. She made a strange, tortured face, then leapt into the woods.

Later, Ned found Claire in the hut. "Her life mate was killed in the attack," Ned explained.

"I'm sorry. I didn't know," Claire said. Now *she* felt guilty. But she knew the fighting hadn't been her fault. It hadn't been the guard's fault, either.

Claire found the time harder and harder to pass, with all the nasty looks the Skinwalkers gave her. She realized now just how welcoming the Skinwalkers had been at first. Welcoming of their enemy. Now only Ned was still friendly — and even he was quieter than usual. Smiles rarely found their way onto his lips.

At least, Claire told herself, his eyes weren't cold. He still looked at her as if he liked her. As if she wasn't like the other One-Skins.

"When will I be put on trial?" Claire asked.

"Soon enough," Ned replied, frowning. "Don't wish for it sooner."

"Why not?" Claire asked.

"Because they're thinking of doing something they've never done before."

"What's that?"

"They're thinking of killing you."

CHAPTER NINE | **Running Away**

Claire drew in her breath. The Skinwalkers wanted to kill her. Just like the humans killed Skinwalkers. Was the whole world mad?

Claire shivered. If she looked at it from far away, she could see the logic. Her cousin had murdered one of theirs. And then her villagers had killed more of them. Her death would even the score.

But Claire didn't want to die! She wasn't ready yet.

"Don't worry, Claire," Ned told her. "I won't let that happen."

Claire snatched up a twig, then tossed it away from her. "Just how are you going to stop it?" She tried to keep the fear out of her voice.

"I'll talk to the council. I'll convince them," Ned replied. "We believe in paying our debts. You saved my life, and tried to save others."

"They might think you're betraying them. You're siding with a human," Claire said, shaking her head. "Your people could come after us both."

Claire could see it in her mind. They'd both be outlaws — running from Skinwalkers and from villagers. Sooner or later Ned would miss his family, his own kind. He might even blame her for the loss.

"I don't care," Ned said. "They won't kill me — or you." The words were certain, but something in his voice was not.

"No." Claire shook her head again. "I won't let you do it."

What they needed was a truce between their two people. It wasn't enough to wish for it, or to just be peaceful on their own. She had to get the villagers to stop seeing Skinwalkers as enemies. To stop killing them. Then the Skinwalkers would have no reason to strike back. But she had to find a way to do it herself. She couldn't risk the Skinwalkers turning on Ned. If he cared about her, they might see it as a betrayal. No, she had to do it alone — and soon.

"I'll fix things," Ned said firmly. "Leave it to me."

Easy to say, Claire thought. But each day she'd felt the Skinwalkers' growing anger.

Still, Claire nodded. She pretended that she was giving in. Ned nodded back. Claire wiped her palms on her tunic. She had to act soon. She had to do something before Ned got in trouble with his own people.

Claire watched the evening take over the forest. The sky deepened. Birds stopped singing, flowers closed, crickets began to chirp. The Skinwalkers blended in with the shadows. Claire lay on the moss beside Ned. She kept her breathing slow and even, pretending she was asleep. But she couldn't sleep — she had a plan.

Only when the camp stopped rustling did Claire dare to open her eyes. She waited many long moments, then glanced over at Ned. The moonlight shone on his pale skin.

Slowly, Claire stood. Careful not to make a sound, she crept out of the hut. Then she looked back. Ned hadn't stirred.

Grateful but sad, Claire crept out of the camp. She'd kept watch when they'd moved again. She was pretty sure she could find her village. She went in that direction,

careful to be quiet. Once she was far enough away from the Skinwalker camp, she moved at a faster pace.

Claire walked, looking up at the stars at times, trying to find her way. The moon was bright enough that she could see where she was going. She'd never been out alone in the woods at night before, but it felt peaceful to her. A good place. Maybe she should have let Ned speak for her. Or run away with him.

But no — those ideas would never have worked. The Skinwalkers would have turned on Ned. The humans would have turned on them both. And Claire couldn't just leave her grandfather. Not forever.

Claire pushed her hair out of her eyes. She didn't know yet how she would talk to the villagers. She didn't know how to end their hatred of the Skinwalkers. But she knew she had to find a way.

Bushes rustled behind her. Claire's heart clenched. She didn't have a weapon, not even her bow and arrow.

Claire bent down and picked up a stone, then another. She tore a strip from her tunic, then tied them together to make a rough slingshot. She was ready, but nothing attacked. Once again the quiet of night drew around her.

Claire walked on, more quietly this time. She heard another rustle, closer by. Then there was the sound of someone breathing.

Someone was tracking her!

Claire spun around, stone in her slingshot, ready to shoot — and Ned pushed through the bushes, grinning at her. His human eyes twinkled at her. His knotted necklace hung at his throat. "You didn't think you were leaving without me, did you?"

"Ned!" Claire spluttered, lowering her slingshot. "I could have killed you!"

Ned grinned wider. "But you didn't."

"How did you find me? You were sleeping — "

"Deer have good ears," Ned replied, winking at her. "I woke up when you were leaving."

"But you didn't try to stop me."

"I knew you'd fight me," Ned said. "So there was no point. Now maybe you'll tell me — where are we going?"

Claire drew a deep, shaky breath. "I don't think you'll want to come along. I'm going back to the village."

"To the village?" Ned frowned. "Why?"

"I want to make them see that you're not the enemy. I want to try to stop the fighting."

"Then you'll need me," Ned said quietly.

Claire shuddered. "No! If they find out you're a Skinwalker . . . ."

"They'll kill me?" Ned said, a crooked smile on his

lips. "I live with that every day. But if you're going to try to make peace, then so am I."

"Ned — " Claire said.

Ned shook his head firmly. "I'm coming."

He'd already followed her in the dark. Claire knew that even if she ran and tried to lose him, he'd follow. As a deer, he could run a lot faster and farther than she could. And his sense of smell and his hearing were so much better than hers.

"Very well," Claire grumbled. But even though she was angry and afraid, she couldn't hold back a smile. Ned was still by her side.

~

They walked quietly all night. Crickets and owls surrounded them with their night music. Claire found it peaceful, walking with Ned. Sometimes they talked, sometimes they simply walked in silence.

Just as the sun began to rise, they heard metal pounding on metal and a woman calling out to a child. They smelled the wood smoke of the village houses and bakery. Soon Claire could see the darkened wood of the village houses.

Claire's throat tightened. She was home.

Claire glanced over at Ned. "You don't have to do this," she said.

Ned raised his head sharply, his eyes fierce and determined. "I want to."

He changed smoothly into human form, the change looking natural. Then he knelt down and pulled a folded cloth out of a tree hollow. He flapped the cloth open, and it became a long tunic which he pulled on to hide his nakedness. "There. How do I look?"

His brown eyes were so big and soft that Claire thought she could lose herself looking into them. Ned looked more innocent and open than the villagers did. And he looked so handsome that Claire's heart hurt.

But he was a Skinwalker. At least a part of him was a deer.

"You look good. Presentable," Claire said.

"You think I'll pass?"

"Yes," Claire whispered.

"Good." Ned lifted the necklace off his neck, and put it on Claire.

"What's that for?" she asked, her eyes widening.

"It's so you know that I like you," Ned told her. "So that everyone knows. Just in case anything happens."

"Nothing's going to happen!" Claire said. But she wasn't sure of her own words.

CHAPTER TEN | The Mob

The village was just waking up. The blacksmith was stoking his fire. The village baker had made his first loaves of bread. The merchants were setting up their carts on the dirt streets. Soon the town would be crowded with people. With One-Skins.

"We'll go to my grandfather's first," Claire whispered.

"Are you sure?" Ned asked.

From around one corner came a person they both knew. Maybe the last person they wanted to see that morning.

"Claire!" Hab shouted. "How did you get here? How did you escape?" He put down the wooden bucket he was carrying. "And who's that with you?"

Claire tried to smile. She hoped Hab wouldn't recognize Ned. She needed to come up with a story. "This is my friend, Ned. When I . . . uh, escaped, he found me in the woods. We've been walking all night to get home."

"Nice to meet you," Hab replied. He clapped Ned's shoulder.

Ned looked startled, like he wasn't used to being greeted that way. But he recovered quickly. "And you, my friend."

"It wasn't hard to get away," Claire went on. "They weren't really guarding me at all. I just walked out but didn't know where I was . . . "

Hab wasn't listening. He wasn't even looking at Claire. His eyes were focused on Ned. "Don't I know you from somewhere?" Hab asked. "You seem — " Then Hab's eyes widened. He turned to Claire. "Oh, no, you didn't. Tell me you didn't."

Claire knew they were in trouble. Hab had seen right through her lies. He'd recognized Ned. He knew exactly how she'd gotten to the village. With one shout, he could bring angry villagers running.

"Ned helped me get home. He'd never harm anyone here," Claire said, touching Hab's arm. "He wants peace between us, just like I do."

Hab shook his head, backing up. "This isn't right. Bringing one of them to our village. After all the men that got killed."

"We just want to live quietly, to be able to go about our lives," Ned said. His eyes were pleading with Hab to understand. "We Skinwalkers also lost many of our own."

Hab looked around him, like he wanted to call out to someone for help.

"Hab, please," Claire cried. "I know my grandmother was kind to you. My mother, too. I know you didn't want them to die. Ned is every bit as good a person as they were. Don't start something here."

Hab swallowed noisily. "No, of course not." He nodded, ducking his head. He didn't look Claire in the eyes very long.

"Thank you." Claire squeezed his arm.

"You sure you know what you're doing, girl?" Hab asked.

"I'm following my heart. How can that be wrong?" Claire replied. "Come on, Ned," she said. "Let's get going."

She hurried Ned down the dirt path between some houses.

Ned looked over his shoulder at Hab. "Do you think he'll keep quiet?"

"I hope so." But Claire wasn't at all sure. She sped up her pace, Ned close beside her.

~

They soon reached her grandfather's house. The small house was dark, despite the morning light streaming through a small window. Bread was set out on the table. But Claire didn't see her grandfather.

"Papa?" she said, stepping into the dark hut. She peered into the gloom.

"Claire!" An old man rose out of the shadows. He took shuffling steps until he reached her. Then he pulled her into a tight hug, almost crushing the air out of her. Claire's grandfather might be old, but he was still strong. "I thought you'd never come home. When that lousy cousin of yours came home without you . . ."

Claire smiled. "I *chose* to stay, grandfather. I was trying to make things better." She squeezed him again, then let him go. "I have someone I want you to meet." She tugged Ned's arm to pull him over. "This is Ned."

Claire's grandfather clapped him on the shoulder. "Well met, young man."

Claire's grandfather studied Ned closely, taking in his huge brown eyes and the gentleness of his face. Somehow he knew, just with a look.

"You're one of them, aren't you, boy? One of my dear wife's people."

Ned looked at Claire for help. He wasn't sure what this meant.

"Don't worry, boy," Claire's grandfather said. "You're very welcome here. I'm not like those others."

Ned smiled, his grin widening until it stretched across his face. "Thank you, sir. You used to walk the woods and leave presents for us, didn't you?"

The old man's face flushed. "I expect you thought it was a silly thing to do."

"No, sir! Not at all. You gave us hope for the human race. We kept hoping there would be more like you."

"Did I, now!" For a moment, the old man looked pleased, almost proud. Then his eyes clouded. "I'm not so sure that's a good thing. Not with the way humans are acting." He shook his head and sighed. "But you two must be hungry. Come, sit down."

He broke some bread into three pieces and poured some water into mugs.

Claire and Ned had taken only a few bites of bread before they heard shouting and running footsteps.

"What are those fool people doing now?" Claire's grandfather muttered. He shuffled to the open doorway, wiping the crumbs from his mouth. He peeked out, then yanked his head back inside. Quickly he slammed the door shut, his old hands fitting an iron bar across the door.

Claire rushed to help him. "What is it?" she asked.

"The villagers," her grandfather said. "They've got

torches and pitchforks, and they're making their way here." The old man looked at Claire, his face deeply lined with worry. "Did you tell anyone about your friend?"

Claire clenched her fists. "Hab recognized Ned, but I didn't think he'd say anything. He said he'd keep our secret."

"He'd feel he had to do his duty, though. He'd try to protect the villagers," Claire's grandfather replied. He blew out his breath. "I think we're in trouble."

They could all hear the villagers now, yelling and banging, stomping on the ground. "Give up the Skinwalker! Give up the monster!"

CHAPTER ELEVEN | Bewitched?

Ned stood slowly. "I'll go out there. It's me they want."

"No!" Claire cried, gripping his arm. "They'll kill you! I won't have that."

Claire's grandfather shook his head. "We won't go losing another one of you to their petty fears. If I'd been here when they took my wife, my daughters. . . ." He turned his head, suddenly looking older. "I would have fought them or run away with my girls if I had to."

"We can't just stay inside here," Ned said. "They

know I'm with you. And if I'm killed — " Ned looked at them unhappily — "my kind will try to get my body home. Failing that, they'll fight to the death. All of us will lose more people."

Claire knew that was true. And she'd made this happen. She should have sent Ned home and come by herself. But she had wanted him with her, and that had been foolish.

"Stay here," Claire ordered him. "No matter what happens, stay here. I won't let them hurt you."

"But — "

"This time, listen to me."

Claire would talk to the villagers, reason with them. She didn't know yet what she'd say, but she knew she had to say something.

Claire grabbed the edge of the open window and hauled herself out. She fell onto the ground, then stood up, brushing the dirt off her. Standing as tall as she could, she walked around the house.

The villagers stood clumped together, yelling, their faces red. Some of them held torches, their black smoke trickling into the air. Others held weapons — pitchforks, knives, clubs, whatever they could find.

Looking at them, Claire felt small and alone. But she straightened her shoulders and stood between the house and the mob. "Shame on you!" she yelled as loudly as she could.

The crowd quieted for her.

Claire went on. "The Skinwalker boy — my guest — has never done a thing to any of you. He is a man of peace, as all of you used to be. Go, and leave us alone!"

There was a noise in the crowd, and then Kelsey came forward. "That's not Claire talking!" Kelsey yelled. "The Skinwalkers have bewitched her!"

"We have to break the spell!" another man yelled.

The villagers began pumping their torches and pitchforks up and down in the air.

Claire felt cold, though the sun shone warmly down on her. "I'm not under any spell, cousin!" she shouted. "No more than you are!"

But the crowd grew louder and more restless.

Claire knew she had to calm the group. But how? She took a step forward. "This madness has gone on long enough. Three years ago, when my grandfather was away, you watched while Hab's father killed my grandmother, my mother, my aunt. Surely you remember. They were good women!" She scanned the crowd, focusing on one face. "Remember, Alice, when my grandmother brought you bread when you had none?"

The woman, Alice, bowed her head.

Claire focused on another face. "Or you, Hab, when my mother nursed your child back to health?"

Hab stopped yelling. The crowd got a little quieter.

"If you condemned them, then you condemn me, because I loved them all. They were kind human beings, and yes, they were also Skinwalkers." *And God help me, I love another Skinwalker,* she thought. But she might never speak those words.

"So you can kill me now, as my family was killed before. You can kill the Skinwalker. But this will not bring peace, nor will it free you from fear. You are better than that, all of you. I know that because I'm one of you. And I know the hatred must end."

The crowd stood silently, watching her. But Claire didn't know what else to say. "Go home, now!" Claire shouted. "Go home before you do something you'll regret for the rest of your lives! We've all seen enough violence. Go home and know you've done the right thing."

The crowd muttered. People shifted and turned. Weapons lowered.

Hab gazed at Claire. He looked ashamed. "I'm going home," he said loudly. "And I suggest you all do the same."

He turned to go. So did Alice, the woman Claire had

singled out. Soon others were leaving as well.

Claire stood there, watching them, hardly able to believe her good luck. Hope surged through her.

Then there was a thump behind her. It sounded like something heavy had fallen. Claire spun around to see Ned walking toward her, still in his human form. He brushed dirt and twigs off his clothes as he walked.

"Didn't I tell you to stay put?" she hissed. But at the same time, she was glad to see him.

When Ned appeared, the crowd grew excited. Some were curious, some afraid. Many made the sign of the cross.

"Who is the stranger?"

"Is that him? The Skinwalker?"

Ned came to stand at Claire's side.

"Hello, good people," he said. "I am the Skinwalker that Claire and her grandfather are protecting. I promise you, I mean no harm."

The villagers began talking among themselves. Hab turned back, joining the crowd again.

Claire licked her dry lips. She smiled at Ned, knowing the crowd was watching her. "Ned saved my life many times over," she said loudly. "He stood up for me when he didn't have to. He is a true friend. I hope you'll all treat him that way."

Claire looked at the villagers' faces. Some looked thoughtful, some scared. Many looked confused. But it was a good sign if they were thinking things over.

Claire could feel the tension going down. *Maybe we can win this one*, she thought. *Maybe they'll begin to understand.*

But then Kelsey stepped forward. "What did I tell you? They bewitched her!" her cousin yelled.

"Kelsey, you stop that!" Claire shot back. "You killed a Skinwalker, and by rights they could have killed you, but they didn't! They treated you well!"

"By locking me up, keeping me prisoner?" Kelsey yelled. His eyes were wild, the chords on his neck bulging. Kelsey looked so different from Ned. Her cousin was angry. Ned stood there calmly, as if nothing could make him mad.

Then Ned spoke, his voice so much quieter than Kelsey's. "If my presence here makes you uncomfortable, then I will leave you," Ned told them all. "But I came here hoping for peace. I came here hoping that no more of my people would ever die at your hands. And that no more of your people would die at ours. I know you lost many people — just as we did. Can we not find a way to live together without hurting one another?"

Behind her, the door to the house creaked open.

Claire turned to see her grandfather join them. He put a wrinkled hand on both her and Ned's shoulders. Then he spoke to the crowd. "It's time for peace, people. It's long overdue. You know it in your hearts."

"No!" Kelsey cried. "They've all gone mad! The Skinwalker has bewitched them all!" Kelsey dashed forward, swinging his torch at Ned. The flames touched Ned's cheek, burning him. Ned yelled, leaping back. In seconds, his legs changed to a deer's, then his entire body.

"You see?" Kelsey yelled triumphantly. "You see? He's not even human!"

"You're the one who's not human!" Claire yelled. She shoved Kelsey away from Ned. "He did nothing to hurt you, but still you attacked him. What kind of human are you?"

Kelsey stood glaring at her for a long moment. There was hate and fear in his eyes. His torch cast red light on his face. "You know he's a Skinwalker," Kelsey said. "You've made this happen."

Claire and her cousin glared at each other. Then Kelsey touched his torch to the thatched roof of Claire's grandfather's house.

CHAPTER TWELVE | The Fire

The flames streaked up along the thatched roof, the fire eating the straw.

"There!" Kelsey shouted. "Let's see you protect the Skinwalker now — without a house to keep him in."

Claire tore her gaze away from Kelsey. She stared at the flames on the roof. For a moment, all she could see was her mother and grandmother burning. Then she focused. In front of her was the house her grandfather loved, and it was going up in flames.

She shook herself. "Fire! My grandfather's house is on

fire!" she cried. She ran into the burning house to get a bucket, then ran to the well for water. She would not let this happen. She couldn't let it end like this.

The villagers cried out, throwing down their pitchforks. Any fire was a threat to them all. Men shouted for buckets of water, women and children ran to fetch them. Already sparks had blown to the baker's house. If they didn't put the fire out now, the whole village would burn down. And there would be nothing left worth saving.

Claire ran forward with her bucket of water, throwing the water up on the roof. Beside her, villagers were creating a line from the well to the house. They passed down buckets of water for Claire and her grandfather to toss on the roof. Then Ned joined in. Even injured, he could throw water farther than the others.

But it wasn't going to be enough.

Claire pulled away from the burning building just as the roof collapsed.

Next door, the baker's roof was going up in flames. A wind swept up, catching more sparks and embers. Soon the fire was blowing toward other nearby houses.

Claire and Ned worked hard. It was too late to save her grandfather's house, but not too late to save the village. They kept throwing water onto the fire, sparks stinging their faces.

Ned pulled back. He seemed to be listening to the forest.

"Come on," Claire yelled. "The fire is spreading."

Then Claire followed Ned's eyes. At last she could see them — the deer and wolf Skinwalkers were standing there at the edge of the forest.

"Come brothers, come sisters!" Ned called. "Help us put out the fire!"

The Skinwalkers didn't move.

"You know this human girl saved me. Help me repay my debt!" Ned called, his voice breaking. Another house caught fire.

The Skinwalkers stood for long moments, staring at Ned and Claire. Then, slowly, they began to move. The Skinwalkers knew what had to be done. Some brought their hidden human clothes from the woods, others changed into human form and put on the clothing. In moments, the villagers could no longer tell them apart — aside from the Skinwalkers being strangers to them. Some Skinwalkers ran to soak their cloaks in the water, then slapped the wet cloth against small flames and sparks. Others created another line at the well, filling buckets and bowls, and passing them down.

The villagers and the Skinwalkers worked grimly together, fighting the greedy fire. Claire's grandfather's

house was past saving. The walls had caught fire, and were burning steadily. But still the fire had to be put out.

Claire's lungs burned, her eyes watered from the heat and smoke of the fire. She breathed in smoke, coughing deeply as she worked. But they were making progress. She could tell. She threw another bucket of water onto the collapsed roof. The last bit of flames sizzled and went out.

Claire cheered, then moved to stand in front of the baker's house as she passed her bucket back. The fire there was almost out. Water from the buckets had dampened the other, newer fires.

Claire felt someone standing too close to her. She turned to see Ulric, his human face as stern as ever. His yellow eyes stared at her necklace — the necklace Ned had given her.

Claire swallowed, suddenly nervous. But Ulric said nothing. He simply nodded and turned back to the fire.

Claire looked around her. Humans and Skinwalkers were working side by side, as if they had never been enemies. Soot and ash covered human and Skinwalker faces alike. Everyone had helped save the village today.

When the last flames were out, Hab turned to the villagers and the Skinwalkers. "We did it — we stopped the fire." He paused, then added, "Together! We couldn't have done it without you, Skinwalkers. Thank you for helping to save our village."

"About time we said it!" Claire's grandfather called out.

Villagers and Skinwalkers looked at each other in stunned silence. Then hoarse cheers sounded out.

Claire felt as light as a leaf. Hearts were mending. The hatred was disappearing. Maybe there would be peace after all.

Ned came beside her and squeezed her hand. "We did it," he said. "We really did it!" His voice cracked. "I wasn't sure we could."

Claire laughed. "Then why did you come?"

"For you, of course," Ned said, grinning at Claire. "And for us all."

Claire hugged him tight, then let him go. She wanted to ease the villagers into this slowly. They would need time to get used to the idea of Ned and her being together. But she wasn't going to hide how she felt.

Claire looked over at the blackened, smouldering walls of her grandfather's house. She swallowed the lump in her throat and looked over at her grandfather. He, too, was staring at what was left of his house, a sad expression on his face. "Papa, are you all right?" Claire asked.

Her grandfather turned his head to look at her. Then his sad, weary face broke into a smile. "Of course I'm all right! You're back, safe and sound. That's what matters. We can always rebuild a house." He gently touched her hair, the way he used to when she was little.

Claire kissed his cheek.

"You can stay at my house tonight, Claire. And every night until we rebuild yours," Hab said. "All three of you."

"Thank you!" Claire replied. She'd waited so long for this to happen. Peace between One-Skins and Skinwalkers. It was hard to believe it was here now.

Still, Claire wondered how Kelsey was taking it. She scanned the crowd, looking for him. She didn't see him at first. And then she caught sight of him, crouched at the edge of a cottage. Kelsey's eyes were wild like a cornered animal. Yet this young man was her cousin, her blood. Claire couldn't just give up on him.

She walked over and knelt down in front of him. "It'll be okay, Kelsey," she said. "It's a good thing."

"It's the end of everything!" Kelsey said.

"No." Claire shook her head. "It's the beginning."

Kelsey stared at the ground.

"Can't we be friends again?" she said.

"I thought I wasn't human," he said in a short voice.

"Of course you are," Claire said firmly. "But what you did to Ned — that wasn't fair. I hope you can see that he's a good person. Just as good as your mother or mine. Ned's here to stay. You need to learn to accept him. Everyone else has."

Kelsey looked up slowly, meeting Claire's eyes. "I'm sorry. It was stupid to burn down your house. I don't know what I was thinking. I never meant to hurt you."

Claire nodded. She couldn't say it was all right. But she thought she understood him. Sort of.

"Try to accept Ned," she said. "He makes me happy."

Kelsey smiled twistedly. "I'll try."

"Good." Claire reached out and squeezed his hand. "It'll get easier. You'll see."

Kelsey took a deep breath. "I may as well start now." He walked over to where Ned was waiting. "Welcome to our family," Kelsey said stiffly, as if he were waiting for Ned to reject him.

"Thank you, Kelsey," Ned said, clasping his shoulder. "I think I'm going to like it here."

Kelsey smiled slowly. "It's a good place to live. Even better now that we're not all fighting."

Claire laughed, unable to hold in her joy. She hadn't been sure peace was possible. She still didn't know if this peace would hold. But for the moment, in this village, the battles were over.

If you enjoyed this book,
you'll love the Dragon Speaker series

The year is 1144 and the world's last dragon has returned. The evil Lord Manning plans to use that dragon to rule the kingdom. According to prophecy, only one person can stop him. And that one person is a sixteen-year-old boy.

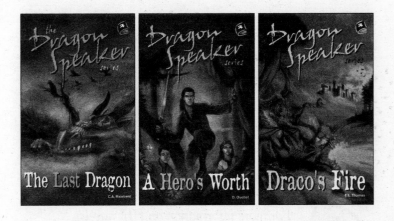

BOOK 1: *The Last Dragon* Jacob, Orson and Lia must rescue the only egg of the world's last dragon.

BOOK 2: *A Hero's Worth* While the young dragon grows, Lia may be forced to marry Lord Manning.

BOOK 3: *Draco's Fire* The fully grown dragon helps Jacob fulfill the prophecy — and rescue his kingdom.

About the Author

C.A. Rainfield is the author of *The Last Dragon* in HIP's Dragon Speaker fantasy series and the much acclaimed young-adult novel *Scars*. She loves to write and read teen fiction — fantasy, magic and gritty realistic novels. For more information, visit her website at www.cherylrainfield.com.

For more information on HIP novels:
High Interest Publishing
www.hip-books.com